To my wonderful sister Lauren and everyone
who has supported me throughout the years.
Thank you – G.W.

To all the inspirational young people, like George,
who glow from the inside out – C.T.

For George, his family and all the wonderful
children like him. Stay magical x – T.B.

Published in the UK by Scholastic, 2023
1 London Bridge, London, SE1 9BG
Scholastic Ireland, 89E Lagan Road, Dublin Industrial Estate, Glasnevin, Dublin, D11 HP5F

SCHOLASTIC and associated logos are trademarks and/or
registered trademarks of Scholastic Inc.

Inspired by an original poem as featured on CBeebies

Text © George Webster and Claire Taylor, 2023
"This Is Me" Poem © Claire Taylor, 2021
Illustrations © Tim Budgen, 2023

The right of George Webster, Claire Taylor and Tim Budgen to be identified
as the authors and illustrator of this work has been asserted by them
under the Copyright, Designs and Patents Act 1988.

PB ISBN 978 0702 31914 3

A CIP catalogue record for this book is available from the British Library.

Printed in China
Paper made from wood grown in sustainable forests and other controlled sources.

1 3 5 7 9 10 8 6 4 2

www.scholastic.co.uk

George Webster
This is ME!

Claire Taylor   **■SCHOLASTIC**   Tim Budgen

This is me, I am George.

My eyes are **sparkly**,
just like my mum.

Like my dad,
I'm **determined**
and **brave**,

and like my sister,
I'm FULL OF FUN!

I have an extra ingredient –
a sprinkling of
magic inside me.

Some people, they say
that I'm special,
but that's not what
I think, you see . . .

We're made of
different ingredients,
that help us **shine**
- like a **star.**

My **glow** is what makes
me who I am,
and **yours** will make
you who you are.

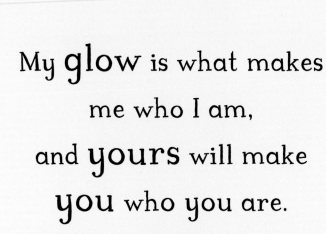

Sometimes, we might need a little help to find out what makes us **glow**.

We can try
new things,

have lots of **fun . . .**

why not give everything a go?

When I was a little bit smaller,
I struggled to make my words clear.

So, I learnt to use my hands to talk
and sign language filled
me with cheer.

My little sis, Lauren, signed with me –
so she could speak **my** special way.

"More food please!"
– that was our favourite.

"More! More! More!"
together we'd say.

There are lots of ways of talking.

We can smile, blink, gaze or shout loud.

However we talk, we need to be heard,
it's what makes us feel bold and proud.

Our differences are **important** –
it's **good** we're not all the same.
The world would be very boring
if everyone had the same name.

Meet **Daniel**
the dreamer,

and **Ruben**
who's strong.

Meet **Francis** – he's cheeky,

and **Louise** who loves a song.

Daniel dreams he's a **model**,

Ruben swims like a **star**.

Francis is a great **dancer**,

Louise, full of **fizz**, will go far.

Each one of us is **different**,
just like pebbles at the seaside.

Together we make a **bigger** splash
and spread our **glow** far and wide.

When I was quite small, I wobbled.

In races, I was rather slow.

But friends, like Roisin, cheered me along,
and now, just look at me go!

I'm a waiter in a café . . .

I love to **dance** . . .

and **cook**.

I like learning with
my best friends . . .

I can even write a book!

My family really help me
to feel I can be ANYTHING.

I dream of being on TV
sharing just what my glow can bring.

There's a **glow** inside each one of us,
in me and every one of you.
Together, we all **shine** much brighter,
and our dreams really **do** come true.

So, when you meet someone like me,
let your **glow** flow all around.
As my extra special ingredient,
could make you feel **up**, not down.

This is me. Yes, I am George.
And I'm **proud** to be me.
So let **your** glow shine through
and be the **best** you can be!